Copyright © 2010 by John Plumb
All rights reserved

The book is dedicated to
my long-lost and then found again
Cindy

A Plumb-line Publication

2

February 15, 1844

The sound of the gavel coming down echoed through the prestigious chamber to signal that the powers to be had reached a decision.

"Mr. Bridges, we have examined your theories of magnetic time travel. The board members of the Royal Society are all in agreement that it is totally insane to think we would give you any money for such a project as this. Now hear me, and hear me well, either you abandon this ridiculous idea or we shall be forced to expel you from the Royal Society. In so doing, we will see to it that you never work in the scientific community ever again. Now what is your answer Mr. Bridges?"

"Mr. MacCullagh, with all due respect to the office of the President of the Royal Society, you seem to leave me no choice. I see no way out except to tender my resignation and move to America. I know that in America I shall be greeted with open arms. Furthermore, I guarantee you, that I shall out live you all by the use of my invention."

The mumbling of all the men in the room was like the under tones of a large engine. In 1844 there were 750 members of the Royal Society and most were in attendance that day.

The Royal Society of London was set up for the Improvement of Natural Knowledge, this oldest society, was known simply as the Royal Society. The society was, and is today, made up of the most knowledgeable people in the sciences. Founded in November 1660, the society was granted a Royal Charter by King Charles II as the "Royal Society of London". The Society was initially an extension of the "Invisible College". The founders intended it to be a place of research and discussion. The Society also acted as a scientific advisor to His Majesty's Government, receiving a grant-in-aid from them, funding a variety of research fellowships and scientific start-up companies. It also acted as the United Kingdom's Academy of Sciences. In the 1703, one of its most notable presidents was Sir Isaac Newton.

However, Mr. Bridges was not to receive such funding. Once all had been said, Charles Bridges gathered up his papers and stormed out of the chamber hall. He did not stop and take the time to shake the dust from his feet.

Once outside, Bridges was quickly approached by a young America man. His name was Martin Hopkins. He had been sent to England as a recruiter and Bridges was the target.

"Mr. Bridges, you mentioned that today you would let me know if you are going to accept Mr. DuPont's offer."

"It looks that way, Hopkins! Tell your boss, Mr. DuPont, that I will need 500 acres and at least $50,000 American dollars."

"Very well sir! I'll get a letter off to him today. How soon would you like me to book you passage on a ship?"

"The sooner I get out of here the better, Hopkins! I have suddenly grown to despise this place."

Charles was a stubborn man in his mid-forties. As far as he was concerned it was his way or no way at all. In his mind he was always correct and he therefore spoke with authority on every subject. He was overweight because he always over indulged. Meat and potatoes were his favorites and were prepared in abundance because his landlady felt that more was a sign of prosperity. He had shaggy, dark-blonde hair that was thinning at the top. His attire was at least 5 years out of date. The only part that showed wear however was the seat of his pants. Years of sitting working on scientific endeavors wore out both clothing and hair by his constant pulling at it when in thought.

He knew his invention would work. Money and a place to work were the central problems. Charles had burned through all other sources of funding on his many other 'sure-to-succeed' projects. No one in England was about to give him any money for any reason.

Martin had won the favor of DuPont because of his boyish charm coupled with his bulldog style. Martin's good looks made heads turn. His beautiful, golden-red hair seemed never to be out of place. His figure was described by the women as statuesque, of course in the Greek fashion. His clothes, always in style, did not emit affluence. All said and done, most men envied him and thus resented him.

Charles was the third professional person that he had gathered up for DuPont. It was obvious to young Martin that DuPont was putting together a team of experts. However, the reason was very unclear. He knew nothing of Charles's 'house of time'.

His only job was to find people that matched the qualifications that Mr. DuPont had outlined.

    In the spring of 1844, Charles and Martin could look forward to a peaceful summer crossing to the states. The weather was that year was perfect for the long trip across the Atlantic. The ship and crew were in tip-top shape and ready to take passengers and cargo aboard. The journey was to last about two months allowing Charles time to continue his study of time travel and draw up initial blue prints for his 'house of time'

The <u>Buckinghamshire</u> was the name of the Tall Ship on which they booked passage. The ship itself had just returned from Australia where it had delivered British prisoners to work in the gold mines.

It was August 12, 1844 when the ship landed in Charleston, South Carolina. There was no one to meet them at the pier because no one knew they were coming. As it turns out the letter that Martin had written to Mr. DuPont was aboard the same ship.

At this time Charleston was a bee-hive of activity with the slave trade in full swing. It was not hard to get a carriage to take them both out to the DuPont Plantation with the many slaves working at the docks. In fact, Charleston had at that time a population over 23,000, of which the majority were black. The distance was ten miles from the docks to the plantation. Martin provided Charles with numerous antidotes and stories about Charleston as they travelled.

Meeting Mr. DuPont for the first time, one would think that he didn't have a brain in his head. However, it was the complexity of his personality that made him come across meek and thus seem rather unintelligent. Physically, he was a small man, 5'6" tall and about 120 lbs. His family was from France and this accounted for his slight build. His thin, narrow nose usually had his silk handkerchiefs underneath. He was allergic to the fragrant magnolia trees that populated his plantation.

DuPont's hair was black and graying at the sides giving his profile a distinguished look. However, his clothing, which usually hung from his slight frame, destroyed the picture his profile provided. His shoes were immaculately polished, but his white stockings hung around his ankles. His slender legs, now out of fashion since the time of Louis XIV, kept him from finding a pair that fit. As the years passed, he also was developing a pronounced slouch, due the pressers of running a plantation.

But with his tight-fisted business deals, he had a reputation that was much larger than his physical bearing. His voice carried a lot of weight and respect in and around the community. His business savvy was unmatched and people regarded him as fair but unyielding.

Bridges and DuPont made a very odd and unlikely team to succeed. Charles was however smart enough to remember from where his money was coming and made no comment on their disparate appearance.

"So Mr. Bridges, tell me how this time traveling house of yours works."

"Well sir, think of time not as a straight line but rather a wavy line with equal up and down peaks. It takes five years to go down to the bottom of the wave and five years to come up. The magnetized house with magnetic rods running parallel throughout the inside walls, will enable it to jump from peak to peak. In other words, it will be a ten year jump. After jumping it will be stable for a week and then atomically jump again. This process will continue on and on until the key is removed.

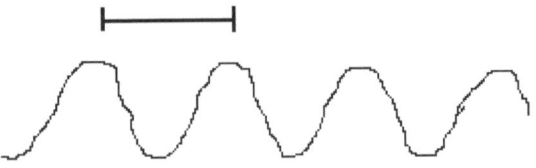

The people in the house will be unaware of the time jump. They will also experience only one day in their life except for the week that it is stable."

"Let me get this straight Mr. Bridges! You're saying that a decade is but a week and that over a forty-year period a person inside the house will only age about a month."

"Yes sir, in forty years only they will only age a month."

"During the week that it is stable we could go out and explore?"

"Yes of course Mr. DuPont. You can go out as long as you are back before it leaps again. That is if you choose to leap again."

"What's it going to take for you to

build this place?"

"I will need plenty of steel and copper rods. Plus quality craftsmen to build the house and it should sit on at least 500 acres so as not to be seen."

"You can construct the house here on my plantation and I shall bring in the finest Dutch carpenters for your employ. Let me ask you, can you build the house with ten bedrooms?"

"Of course whatever you would like, as long as the exterior walls are 10 inches thick."

A month later construction began in the far corner of the plantation. DuPont gave Bridges everything he asked for without question. That is, up until it came time to furnishing the house. That's when DuPont took over. Also unlike most houses of the day, this house was built with the out houses attached. This of course was for obvious reasons.

The magnetized steel rods alternated with the copper rods every 10 inches. They ran parallel from the floor to the top of the second story. The craftsman had bored large holes through the 10 inch upright beams to accommodate the parallel rods.

The beams, which extended twenty feet to the roof, were made of oak and quit strong. It was constructed like a balloon style house of the day. All the copper and steel rods were connected at one location in the house and when the final bar, which was called the key, was installed the house would be activated.

According to Charles's calculations the key had to be installed at 6 a.m. on September 3, 1845. This would be the peak moment of the time wave. The house would then reappear on August 27th every ten years and disappear again on September 3. DuPont bought and extra 40 slaves to get the house built on time. All the slaves spoke only Gullah and so DuPont hired a foreman by the name Samuel Carson who spoke the slave language. This way he could insure that the slaves understood the directions and that he could be informed of the slaves' conversations.

It was crucial that nothing ever be built on that same location. Even Bridges himself could not imagine what the consequences would be. DuPont had a ten-foot-high stone wall built 40 feet away from the four sides of the house. An iron gate leading in was also added and it was to be permanently locked.

Chapter 2
All Aboard

On September 1, 1845 DuPont broke the news to Mr. Bridges that he was not going on the first run of the house. Charles was convinced that it was from fear of what might happen to the people in the house that made DuPont opted out of the adventure. However, DuPont assured him that is was because he had many things to set up for the future of the project.

DuPont belonged to a secret society and he told many of the members of his house of time. He made them vow not to speak of it to anyone. Several of the individuals to whom he told expressed an interest in going, several being four men.

Two of the men were married and wanted to bring their wives and another was single. The forth was married and did not wish to bring his wife.

Samuel Carson also signed up to go and brought two young Negros with him: one male, one female. They were to cook and clean. This made a total of nine people to go on the first ten-year run.

Eight months into building the house two things happened. First, Martin Hopkins had got married; and secondly, he found out about the project. So on the evening of September the 2nd Martin showed up with his new wife, Elizabeth. They both insisted on going.

This took Bridges and DuPont by surprise. Martin had been kept out of the loop and at first they didn't know how he discovered what had transpired since Charles' arrival. The answer was in reality simple; Elizabeth's father was a member of the secret society.

She and Martin overheard a conversation that took place between her father and another member in her father's parlor. Permission was granted for them both to come aboard. However, her father knew nothing of her leaving. Now there were twelve of them to take the first leap.

No one really knew if the house was going to work; not even its inventor. If it did not work it would then be known as an $82,000 folly which was about a third of DuPont's net worth.

DuPont let it be known that he wanted to watch the house disappear. Bridges warned him that he could not actually watch because there would be a bright flash of light, much like a lightening flash, that might blind him. Charles instructed him to stand behind the stone wall and when he heard the sound of thunder then he could look. DuPont then looked at Bridges and said, "See you in ten years!"

Bridges then said, with a big smile, "And I shall see you Mr. DuPont tomorrow!"

Anticipation was high for this first attempt. Everyone in the house was gathered in the parlor. Next to the fireplace a section of the wall was not yet in place.

This was the location of the last piece that had to be put in place to activate the house into its time travel mode. The key was especially made and it had to fit in just so.

It was 5:30 a.m. and at exactly 6:00 a.m. Bridges was to put the key in place. Every heart was fiercely pounding and it felt like their hearts were in their throats. All eyes were affixed on Charles as he snapped the key in place.

At that moment they were glad that they still had the oil lamps on because everything went dark. There was no more morning sun. The windows were blackened as if they had been white washed with black paint.

DuPont, on the other hand, did in fact see a bright light shine through the gate and it was immediately followed by a loud cracking sound. For the next three minutes he experienced a ringing in his ears. However, after the loud crack, he peered through the gate; and, sure enough the house was gone.

Chapter 3
The First Ten

Unlike the people on board the house, DuPont had much work to do before he could even think about going on the next trip into the future. He needed to make certain that the 500 acres that the house would land on would be protected throughout time. Using his exceptional wisdom and his ability to influence people, DuPont decided to start another secret society. This one would be made up of just common men. It was his judgment that common men could be manipulated into maintaining the property as part of their membership. Being a member of the southern aristocracy, the belief that the common man was incapable of anything but 'common' thoughts and ideas was second nature to him. Wealth meant that a person was above everyone in thought and privilege. How else could one account for their wealth?

He would call this new society the Protectors of the Light or PTL for short. DuPont built a meeting hall, or lodge as some called it, on the 500 acres. He deeded the land to the society. He then set up levels of knowledge that the members could aspirer to and allow them to know more about the house. Only the top three members in the PTL would know the whole truth. He had long hoped that Martin would run the society and recruit new members to keep it going. This of course was no longer possible.

DuPont then had a large granite slab made with two marble angels on either end. He placed it inside the stone wall area on the far back wall, straight across from the steel gate. On the slab was engraved, "In Memory of Winston DuPont." He told the members of the PTL that it was his father's marker. Then he assigned the task of maintaining it to the PTL in exchange for the land.

He set up a pass phrase for people to say in order to be allowed to come visit the marker. The phrase was: "Mr. Bridges sent for me!"

In the meantime, DuPont's plantation was producing well. The cotton, peanuts and pecans were once again building up DuPont's bank account. However, the last three years before the house was due to return, he started to convert his holdings into gold coins. He knew that even in the future precious gold could be used as money.

Mr. DuPont was not the only one that had his hands full, Bridges had his full with the guests. Moments after the house took off, Peter Blake, the man that did not bring his wife, broke out a bottle of whiskey. He was wearing a dark blue suit with alligator boots.

The story that he told was that he had killed the alligator himself for the boots. He also claimed that before killing the 12 footer it bit off his big toe on the right foot. At one time he was a well-off land owner until alcohol consumption allowed it to slip al away.

He stated that he was glad that he did not have to be there when his wife died. It turns out that she was dying of consumption and only had a few months to live.

At that time many people died of consumption. Consumption was the most common disease of the day. If a person contracted consumption the body wasted away, the person spit up blood and racked with terrible coughing fits. It was also accompanied by high fever.

The other members of the house were shocked to hear that he did not wish to be with his wife in her hour of need. Not to mention that he would not be attending her funeral. They all came to find out later that Peter only cared about money and whiskey and had no room for anything else.

The single fellow, by the name of James Witty III, joined in with Peter by having a drink to celibate their departure. James was a spoiled twenty-two year old boy and was running away from his domineering father. He felt that his father was thrusting too much responsibility upon him. He would much prefer to chase after the ladies.

Sidney Liggett, another time traveler was in his mid-fifties and with his money he attracted the attention of Julie whom he had married. Julie was a slender and spunky 25-year-old gold digger from Atlanta. Unlike women of the day she wore her hair down. This allowed Julie to show off her shimmery golden locks. She often wore a single ribbon, matching the color of her dress, to hold her hair back out of her deep blue eyes. She did not have to wear makeup of any kind. Her checks had a natural glow and her lips were full and pink. A natural beauty, she was aware of this beauty and flaunted it every chance she had.

Sidney her husband was overweight and his health was on the downward spiral. It was from a combination of cigars, rich food and sitting at the poker table. Although aware of his wife's flirtations, he outwardly showed little concern. He made up for his degradation and jealousy by the large quantities of food he ate and being unable to stop his gambling.

Timothy Bean and his wife Sarah were also running away. But their reason was debt. Timothy had started a ship building company and had disappointed one too many customers. Their hope was to get a new, clean start twenty years into the future. Even though Tim was a failure at business Sarah worshiped the ground on which he walked on. Because she was a buxom woman she commanded a wide berth.

Samuel Carson felt justified coming along to keep the Negro's in line. Sam was a strong man. He hand arms like tree stumps. It was apparent to all that his knowledge of the world was limited to brute strength and his ability with a whip. His wardrobe was not much nicer than the slaves' he was to watch over.

Other than the blacked-out windows there was no indication that the house was moving or unstable in any way. Shortly after takeoff Sidney Liggett tried his best to get a poker game started but there were no takers. So he amused himself by playing a type of solitaire.

During the casual sit down lunch Julie Liggett and James Witty sat across from each other. Many glances and half smiles were exchanged by the two of them. Directly after lunch Peter staggered to his room and passed out drunk.

Martin and his wife Elizabeth, for the most part, kept to them self. However, Martin felt closest to Mr. Bridges than any of the other guests because he had known him when he still lived in England. Plus, he was the one that helped bring him to this country.

The biggest topic of discussion turned into a game: "What is the world going to be like the next morning?"

Of course Sidney tried his best to get everyone to wager on their thoughts. There was also much discussion on whether to jump again or get off. Most agreed that they would determine their travel plans during the week of discovery.

The male Negro hand been a field hand and the evening meal was to be a formal affair. So Sarah with the aid of Samuel tried to teach the male Negro how to be a server during dinner. They did manage to get him marginally adequate for the position.

Dinner was to be at seven o'clock sharp. Peter arose at six only to come down and start sipping on another whiskey. He stared at the blackened parlor window and, if you looked closely at him, you could see his eyes tearing up. Could it be that he was showing remorse for what he had done to his wife by leaving her alone?

The house only moved forward; so there was no turning back for anyone. Most did not want to go back. Charles fantasized about going back to England and bragging about his success to the Royal Society.

However, he had no intention of leaving his house for more than the week it was stationary.

The evening meal featured prime rib served with horseradish and an 1835 Graham's Port, bottled in Portugal. After dinner Martin's wife, Elizabeth, played the piano while the others sipped on brandy.

Gems of American Life.

The piano was a Steinway that resonated through the entire house. She played songs of the day such as: "Farewell Is a Lovely Sound" and "My Happy Home." Elizabeth had played the organ for the local Episcopal Church. She was sure to be missed. Elizabeth, although average in every way, was exceptional in her ability to play the organ and the piano.

DuPont had spared no expense in furnishing the house. His goal was to express an atmosphere of wealth and prestige. Carson knew that he did not fit in with the décor.

They were all anxious to retire for the night. Tomorrow would determine if in fact they had transported themselves ten years into the future.

Mr. Bridges himself took on the task of waking everyone up at 4:45 a.m. As they gathered in the parlor at 5:45 many tried to wear a smile but it was obvious that most were nervous. No one knew what to expect so they just stared at the windows.

Chapter 4
The Return

At 6:00 a.m. on August 27, 1855, in less than a blink of an eye, the stone wall that was forty feet away suddenly appeared with the morning sun. A sigh of relief came over everyone except the Negroes who knew nothing of the trip that they had just taken.

The next question was what was the date? So far Bridges had been right about everything. Carson was the one that ran over and opened the sealed front door. Standing there was a much older DuPont and three other wide-eyed men. With a huge smile DuPont walked in and said, "Welcome home!" Then after a warm welcome hand shake to each traveler he gave them all a hand written paper of the major events of the past ten years.

Events

1846 Wilmot Proviso attempts to ban slavery in the West

1848 Mexican War ends and Zachary Taylor elected President of the United States and the Free-Soil Party forms

1849 California and Utah request admittance to the Union

California was admitted to the Union as a free state (Utah was not admitted because the Mormons refused to give up the practice of polygamy).

1850 Compromise of 1850 Congress passes Fugitive Slave Act

The fate of slavery in the other territories, though, would be determined by popular sovereignty. Next, the act of slave trading (though not slavery itself) was banned in Washington, D.C. additionally; Texas had to give up some of its land to form the New Mexican territory in exchange for a cancellation of debts owed to the federal government.

1850 Taylor dies; Millard Fillmore becomes president

1852 Harriet Beecher Stowe publishes Uncle Tom's Cabin and Franklin Pierce was elected President of the United States

1853 Gadsden Purchase negotiated

1854 Ostend Manifesto exposed

1855 William Walker invades Nicaragua

The house itself had held up fairly well. The white washed paint job looked lightly sand blasted and a few shingles were missing. Carson and the male Negro saw to the repairs.

With all the news circling in their heads, the rest of them could not wait to get out and explore how the world had changed. Julie shouted, in what could be described as a childish voice, "Let's go everyone we only have a week." She of course was assuming everyone was going on the next trip. She then bounced out the door to gather up the sunshine.

While traveling into town, disappointment soon set in when they discovered that not much had changed. Charleston had somewhat grown in population and size and different clothing was in style. But overall it was business as usual.

Peter's wife of course was dead and he did take the time to visit her grave. Before leaving the house they were all cautioned about visiting relatives. Bridges and DuPont felt that the relatives would ask too many questions about where they have been and why they had not aged. However, two of them did not take that advice to heart.

One of them was James Witty III. When he left the house he headed straight over to see his father. The meeting with his father did not go well. After hearing where he had been for the last ten years his father yelled, "James!" You're a lazy, no good son and taking the easy way out of life."

"You're just jealous of my new-found fountain of youth and you wish you had come along."

With that being said James Witty the II pulled out his side arm and said, "Get out of here before I put an end to your youth!"

Elizabeth was the other one that did not take the advice of Bridges and DuPont. Martin, her husband, was content to stay and talk with DuPont about all the political things that had transpired; but, Elizabeth was not. She told Martin that she was going shopping with Julie. However, she went directly to her father's house.

The meeting with her father also did not go well. He was torn between being glad to see she was alive and his anger toward his son-in-law for taking his little girl away from him. He was also angry at DuPont for allowing her to take apart in his hair-brain idea of time travel.

"Father if I had told you, you would have tried to stop me!"

"You're right! A woman's place is in the home. Not out seeking adventure with your low life husband!"

With tears running down her cheeks she swiftly fled out of the house. After Elizabeth was gone her father thought more about DuPont, and the more he thought the more his anger turned into rage. He also mistakenly assumed that the experiment was over and he had his daughter back.

Later that week Bradley, Elizabeth's father, discussed the horrible episode with other members of their Secret Society. They concluded that he should challenge DuPont to a dual. DuPont caught wind of the impending challenge and decided that it would be in his best interest to stay in the house of time until they left into the future. He would then contend with Bradley ten years from now.

DuPont got word to his personal Negro to get the bags he had packed and take them to the threshold of the house grounds where the PTL were standing guard. The threshold was a ten minute horseback ride from the house through the woods. DuPont was counting on the fact that Bradley would not discover his where about.

The plantation was turned over to the PTL to run and they were allowed to keep half the profit for the next ten years until DuPont returned. In his mind DuPont thought he had covered all the bases. Little did he know what would happen while he was gone.

Martin was content to stay in the house and talk with the three men of the

PTL. They were the ones that were awe struck by the sudden appearance of the house. Although having some knowledge of the house because of their membership, what they saw was beyond comprehension; a house had materialized out of thin air.

Martin knew nothing of his wife's trip to see her father. That was not the only secret being kept from him. All of the guests of the house for one reason or another unanimously decided to take at least one more trip into the future. Samuel Carson had also decided to stay but not before going over to his water-front bars and shooting off his mouth about the house. This began the legend of the House of Time, which was to live on until the present.

On the morning of September 3rd 1855 at 6:00 a.m. the house automatically left. It simply left on its own. For the first time DuPont experienced the blackened windows. There were now thirteen guests aboard.

This time they were all more relaxed and in a party mood. The whiskey and wine flowed while Elizabeth played some lively songs on the piano, if you can imagine that being done.

As the day went on there was more and more speculation about the upcoming week.

Chapter 5
The Second Coming

On August 27, 1865 the house once more reappeared. As the blackened windows revealed the sunlight DuPont discovered that the yard had not been tended to. It was apparent that the PTL had let him down. They all walked outside except the Negroes that were left to clean up.

They noticed that the gate was open and one hinge was broken. There was no one from the PTL to greet them with transportation to explore and move around Charleston. It was a long walk to DuPont's esquire mansion. The entire plantation was over grown. It looked like nothing had been attended to in years. You cannot imagine the look on DuPont's face when he saw his ransacked house. Plus, there were several families of Negroes living in it. The travelers obtained some horse and buggies and rode into Charleston.

The group was shocked and mortified by what they saw. Utter destruction was everywhere. They did not know where to go to get answers to the horrific destruction they saw. What few questions they dared ask revealed that there had been a war. There was still a strong presence of soldiers throughout the ruins of the city.

DuPont figured the best place to go get answers was the Charleston weekly Gazette. There he discovered that the slaves had been freed and that his plantation was given over to Negro share croppers. Joseph Guerin had complied an article that summed up what had happened with their town.

On December 20, 1860, after the election of Abraham Lincoln, the South Carolina General Assembly made the state the first ever to secede from the Union. Then on January 9,

1861, Citadel cadets fired the first shots of what became the American Civil War by opening fire on the Union ship *Star of the West* entering Charleston's harbor. April 12, 1861, shore batteries under the command of General Pierre G. T. Beauregard opened fire on the Union-held Fort Sumter in the harbor. After a 34-hour bombardment, Major Robert Anderson surrendered the fort. The southern states after a brutal four years eventually lost the war and the slaves were freed. The entire south lay in ruins and hundreds of thousands were dead. He went on to say, in 1865, Union troops moved into the city, and took control of many sites, such as the United States Arsenal, which the Confederate army had seized at the outbreak of the war. The War department also confiscated the grounds and buildings of the Citadel Military Academy.

DuPont set out to find surviving members of the PTL. He was able to find 9 of the 53 with whom he had started. One of them was a top ranking key member. As good fortune would have it the 500 acres were still under control of the PTL. DuPont took the rest of the week rebuilding his Secret Society.

James Witty III discovered that his father was dead and that all his business holdings were gone as well. In fact everyone was broke except DuPont who had the foresight to covert to gold.

Elizabeth went home to find that her father who, because of the war, was quite ill and spiritually a broken man. While she was in town, behind Martin's back, she went to a doctor to confirm that she was indeed pregnant. Once her instincts had become fact, she went to Martin and explained that they had to stop time jumping.

Martin became outraged and told her that there was no way he was going to stay in this post-war environment. Elizabeth was determined not to be like Peter and abandon her family in their time of need. However, Elizabeth gave in and went back to the house.

Then the night before they were to leave she snuck out at two o'clock in the morning and returned to her father's home. By the time Martin awoke it was too late to retrieve her and still make the jump. So he decided to jump without her.

Timothy and Sarah saw the devastation as an opportunity to start over. With nothing left in Charleston anyone with ambition could be able to make a go of starting a new business. It was the perfect opportunity for Timothy to begin to build ships again and help the South in their reconstruction. So they gathered up what little they had and stayed behind.

Sidney was now broke and Julie no longer desired to be with him, especially now that Sidney was just another poverty ridden old man. Her eyes turned to young James Witty III.

Samuel Carson saw no need in telling the Negroes they were free. The other guests of the house all agreed with him because they could not imagine life without them.

Charles Bridges, being an Englishman, could have cared less about what had happen to the people of America. He was a self-centered man and all he cared about was that his house was safe.

On September 3, 1865 the house started to travel again. All the guests were there except for Timothy and Sarah Bean and Elizabeth Hopkins and her unborn baby. That night was a somber night. However, Peter used the war as one more excuse to get drunk.

Long about mid-night Julie slipped out of bed and crept into James's room. James of course found her boldness delightful. But after their moments of satisfying each other they both fell asleep in the same and now unclean bed.

In the morning Sidney went looking for his wife. He couldn't find Julie in any of the common areas so he decided to bust into James's room. However, not before he made a quick stop in his bedroom snatching up his pistol. He had not been blind to the fact that Julie fancied James.

The door frame splintered as the weight of an enraged Sidney forcefully slammed into it. Upon hearing the crash the two sat up in bed only to discover an off balance Sidney entering. He aimed his pistol with a wobbly hand at James. Then in a loud baritone voice that the entire house could hear he said, "You scoundrel, I'm going to make you bleed!"

As if he was not fully awake, James with squinty eyes, put his hand up like he was going to stop the bullet with it and calmly muttered, "Wait! It's not my fault!"

With that being said, an enraged Sidney pulled the trigger. The bullet struck James just below his left breast. The only thing that remained to be done now was to hold a memorial service.

Julie was horrified; she rapidly grabbed a sheet and jumped out of the bed.

Sidney simply said, "Get your garments on and meet me downstairs."

In every one's opinion the shooting was justified. This particular morning the house had just landed in 1875. While they all were all sitting down eating breakfast Samuel suggested, "If it would please you I'll have the Negro dig a grave out in the yard."

DuPont followed by saying, "That would be fine. Make sure the bedding gets buried as well."

So it was that the house continued on without a further thought of James. Julie was forced to live with her shame. The rest of the week in 1875 was not without another event.

After six days of contemplation, Martin went looking for his wife Elizabeth. He started looking for her father's old house. The city had changed so much he found it difficult to locate. It was late in the afternoon when his carriage did pull up out front of the ivy-covered home where she was living. He immediately noticed a young boy sitting on a front porch swing reading a book.

Martin's heart started to race in thinking that this boy might be his son. Once on the porch Martin looked at the boy and asked, "What is your name son?"

"Why it's Marty, Sir!"

"Is that short for Martin?"

"Yes Sir it is."

"And your last name is?"

"Vernon. Are you looking for my father?"

"No! I believe I'm looking for your mother. Is her name Elizabeth?"

"Why yes, did you wish to speak with her? She is right inside I shall get her for you."

The few moments that Martin was waiting seemed to be an hour. He was not at all sure of what to say to Elizabeth. But if that was his son then why did he not have the last name of Hopkins? Martin could see that the boy did favor him with his red hair.

A much older and heavier Elizabeth came to the door and her expression was at first a friendly greeting but it quickly turning to a look of shock at seeing Martin. Elizabeth had not aged well.

The years were not at all kind to her. She looked much older than the ten years that had passed. Martin had half expected to find her still young and beautiful.

"My God Martin, what are you doing here?"

"Is that my son?"

"No, that child died! I have remarried and he belongs to my husband Edward."

"You cannot remarry we were never divorced."

"When you left, my father had you declared dead in the war."

"I did not leave, you did!"

"You had your chance Martin. Now get out and leave us alone!"

Martin was certain that Elizabeth was lying about young Marty not being his son.

He then looked at Elizabeth before putting his head down and saying, "Very well I'll leave and I wish you all the best."

Then without looking up turned and walked off the porch. When his last foot was off the steps he heard the door slam shut. Martin looked and saw Marty examining his old carriage. This gave him an idea. He approached the young boy and said, "Marty, how would you like to surprise your mother with a two dollar bill?"

"What would I have to do to earn that much money sir?"

"Well young man I live not too far away and I need help moving my desk from one side of my parlor to the other. Do you think you could help me? I would then bring you right back home and for your kindness you would be two dollars richer."

"Very well Sir. I'd be happy to help you!"

"Good, climb aboard!"

As the carriage was speeding away Elizabeth just happened to look out the upstairs window and saw Marty leaving with Martin. She tried to run downstairs to yell for him to stop but she was too late. The carriage was out of sight.

Elizabeth ran three blocks to get to Edward's law office where she told him that Martin was back and he had kidnapped their son.

Edward asked, "Where did they go? I'll go after them."

In a demanding voice she said, "You'll have to take me with you because you will never find it."

They both immediately jumped in his carriage and put the horse into a full gallop.

As Martin was getting close to the protected 500 acres area, Edward was drawing near. Elizabeth took the reins and Edward pulled out his pistol, a shot rang out. A bullet struck Martin from behind in his right shoulder. If the bullet had been a little bit more to the right in would have hit Marty.

Martin fell forward and Marty looked back and saw that it was his mother and father chasing them. He then picked up the reins and pulled the carriage to a stop.

Soon both carriages came to a stop. Edward jumped out and directed Marty to get in with his mother. For a brief moment he thought about killing Martin. However, he just told him to go back to where he came from and never think about coming back. Then Edward, Elizabeth and Marty rode back to town.

    All the way back home, Marty was full of questions. Martin had told him that he was his real father. Once home Elizabeth broke down and told Marty the whole truth. She explained that Martin was his real father and she even told him about the House of Time. That sobering truth Marty never forgot.

    Martin continued to live in the house of time. However, because of that bullet wound, Martin had lost total and permanent use of his right arm. If he was to keep up with his journal he would have to learn to write left handed.

Chapter 6
The betrayal

Timothy and Sarah had spent the last ten years in Charleston helping to rebuild their lives and the city after the war. He had started a fairly successful construction company. About a year before the house was to reappear in 1875 Timothy had signed a contract to build an apartment building. However, part of the way into the job he ran out of money. The owner and the bank would not advance him any funds. So in desperation he went to a loan shark by the name of Louis Dulbecco a carpet bagger from New York City.

The user fees were high and so were the stakes if he defaulted on the loan which he eventually did. Dulbecco and his boys came calling for the last time on August 26, 1875. This was the day before the house was to reappear.

Louis was not a happy man and that was not good for Timothy. Louis was demanding all his money back with interest or Timothy would disappear for good. Timothy explained that he was once again out of money and could not even make payroll. So he pleaded with Louis to loan him more money. As far as Louis was concerned this was out of the question.

Louis turned toward his two strong armed men and told them to kill Timothy and turn the office upside down to make it look like a robbery. He then turned his sights to Sarah and said sarcastically, "And you little lady, if you breathe a word about who did this to anyone you will be next."

That's when Sarah spoke up and said, "Mr. Dulbecco I'm certain you have heard the stories about the House of Time have you not?"

"So what!"

"It is due to reappear tomorrow morning at 6 a.m. and we know where. If you would just let Timothy live we will take you to see the House of Time for yourself."

"Why should I believe you?"

"It's just one more day and because Timothy and I have traveled in the house."

"Tell you what. If this house really exists and you can get me and my boys on it when it leaves again. I will not only let you both live I will also give you the money you asked for."

So it was that at five o'clock the next morning they were all headed to the stone court yard. Sarah's only concern was that the pass phrase to get by the PTL had not changed.

It turned out that the phrase had not changed and they were allowed to proceed on up to the stone court yard. The three Italians had their bags packed and Dulbecco had one just full of cash. Timothy explained to them about not looking and the bright light and that there would be a loud cracking noise.

Louis threatened them both again; "You better be right or at 6:05 you're both going to be dead!"

As predicted there was a bright flash of light and a loud bang. The house had arrived on time. When DuPont opened the door, Timothy and Sarah were standing there with the three men.

DuPont quickly said, "I see you're back and it would appear that you have brought some unwanted visitors."

Sarah, who had become the domineering one of the two, spoke up and said, "Mr. DuPont these three gentlemen would like to come aboard and travel one time with you."

"Oh, I see you did not bring unwanted visitors: you brought unwanted guests."

"Well Sir, if you hear me out I'm certain this would be not only profitable to them but quite profitable for you as well."

"Then please come in and I will listen."

Even Dulbecco did not know what she was about to say. After sitting in the parlor Sarah said, "Mr. DuPont our friend here Mr. Dulbecco has made a rather large purchase of rare wine that was pressed and bottled on the Thomas Jefferson Plantation. He feels that in another ten years the wine will triple in value. He would be glad to share the profits with you if you allow him and his two associate's safe passage."

"Where is this wine now Mr. Dulbecco?"

"Just north of here, on the coastline Mr. DuPont"

"Very well if you take me there this afternoon and if everything is fine then we will have a deal."

For a moment Sarah thought her lie was going to backfire. As it turned out Louis walked the two out of the house and handed Timothy a stack of money and said, "You should let your wife run your business."

The two of them wasted no time getting on their horses and riding off. DuPont and Bridges showed off the house and then they had coffee while they waited for lunch to be served. While waiting Louis asked many question about the house and about how they were able to keep it a secret for so long. Bridges and DuPont were more than happy to tell them everything about the PTL and even how the house worked. All this proved to be a huge mistake.

Louis persuaded Charles to come with them by enticing him by giving him a bottle of the Thomas Jefferson wine. Bridges just could not walk away from an offer like that. So after lunch the five of them mounted horses and rode off.

About halfway to Charleston, Louis made the announcement that he needed to relieve himself. The five of them stopped and as Dulbecco dismounted his horse his two running mates pulled out their guns and shot DuPont and Bridges dead.

Next they took their bodies and placed them over there saddles and took them deep into the woods and underbrush. Once there they shot DuPont's and Bridges' horses. They then slowly rode back to the House of Time. When they arrived back at the house the two Negroes were outside hanging laundry on the clothes line. Samuel was standing there watching them. Louis walked up to Sam and asked if they were free or still slaves? Samuel said, "They belong to Mr. DuPont."

Dulbecco said, "Well then I guess they're mine now. Mr. DuPont and Mr. Bridges traded me the house for the 20 cases of wine."

"Are they coming back to tell me this?"

"I do not think so. They told me they were going to get a wagon and take them directly to Philadelphia."

Samuel felt betrayed but said no more about it. Louis took up residency in DuPont's old room where he broke into his safe and discovered his stash of gold coins.

Once they had been in 1885 for five days, Peter had become extremely frustrated with not having any money to spend. With twisted wisdom he decided to rob a bank. It was his idea that he could steal the money just as the bank closed on September 2nd. Then he would ride out to the house to hide until it left the next morning and no one would be the wiser.

After his revelation to acquire money, his demeanor around the house brightened up. The only one that noticed it was Julie.

While they both sat in the parlor, Julie was sewing and Peter sipping. For some reason their eyes met and a small smile came to their faces. Julie took the occasion to speak. No one had been talking with Julie since her episode with James.

"Please Sir, take no offence, but I can see it in your eyes, you're up to something."

Peter was on his third whiskey so his lips were loosened. "Yes Julie, I have found away to wrap my hands around a large sum of money."

"Why Mr. Peter by, all means include me in so I can get out and off this dreadful house."

He leaned slightly forward in his chair and lowered his voice and said, "I'm going to rob a bank."

"Mr. Peter, do you need a gun?"

"No Julie but I could use a lookout."

"Count me in, when do we go?"

The two of them plotted out the crime right up to the last detail. At five till five in the evening on September 2nd Julie stood outside the First Bank of Charleston while Peter went inside carrying a large cloth sack. He pulled out his gun and demanded all the cash from the safe. The bank manager and teller did as they were told.

Once Peter had the cash he ran outside and they both mounted their horses and rode off. As planned they did not ride towards the house for fear they might be followed. Once they were about 25 miles from nowhere, Peter came to a stop and told Julie to get off the horse because he wanted to divide up the money. This was not in their plan but Julie went along.

When they had dismounted Peter walked over to Julie and wrestled her to the ground face down. He then bound her hands behind her back. Taking the rest of the rope he tied the other end it to a thirty pound rock. Before leaving her to drag the rock back to Charleston he shot her horse.

Peter rode back to the house with all the money. The next morning the house left on time without Julie, Bridges and DuPont. The ones aboard were Martin, an accused kidnapper, Peter a bank robber, Sidney a murderer, Dulbecco a thief, blackmailer and murderer and his two thugs who were equally as bad. Also included in this array of mismatched people were Samuel Carson and the two Negroes he kept without telling them they were free.

Chapter 7
1885 Here we come!

As the door was opened there stood all three key members of the PTL. With them was of course the newspaper of the day and a list of major events from the past ten years. Bringing the newspaper was became a tradition that DuPont had started.

However the PTL was surprised that DuPont was no longer a guest. The three members were somewhat suspicious of Louis though. However, like the rest of them, they did go along with Louis taking charge.

All the guests of the house, except Martin, left to go explore the new world. Martin's bullet wound was fresh and he was in too much pain it leave. Martin was still nothing more than a young, twenty-six-year-old boy. However, at two o'clock that afternoon he had three visitors come knocking at the door. The visitors were a forty-five-year-old Elizabeth and Marty his son, who was now twenty. With them was another young man that they called Henry. It was Edwards's son from his first marriage who was now twenty two years old. Henry was 5'8 making him much shorter than the 6'1 Marty. Martin was shocked to say the least that Marty had grown so tall. In his eyes it was only yesterday that he was ten years old.

Elizabeth had enough foresight to bring with her a dressing for Martin's wound. She then told him that shortly after they left that two men were found shot to death. They were found by an old man who was hunting.

Apparently they had been murdered. The newspaper described the two men and in the article. It said the sheriff had posted photographs of the two bodies at the sheriff's office. By the newspaper's description it sounded like Bridges and DuPont. So she went down and saw that it was in fact

Bridges and DuPont.

Placing Martin's left hand between her hands she said, "There was no way I could tell them who they were."

Looking up toward the ceiling Martin said, I think I know who killed them. But I don't know why and I certainly do not know what to do about."

There was no way Martin could go to the authorities; but, he did need to tell Carson, Sidney and Peter. However, they were gone and may not come back until just before the house left again.

Marty then flabbergasted Martin by announcing that he and Henry wanted to become guests in the house.

Martin's first reaction was to say no! Then he looked at Elizabeth and asked, "Did you know about this?"

Elizabeth replied, "Yes, and I think they should go with you, especially now."

Henry reacted saying, "We brought guns and we can keep them from coming in."

Martin, a little bewildered said, "What if they come back before the rest of them do? Then what?"

Marty stood up and said, "We can go find them now and bring them back!"

So it was that the search for the other three began. Martin with his injured arm, said that he would go find Carson. He was convinced that Samuel Carson could be found at a waterfront tavern.

Sam was in fact in his favorite tavern shooting of his mouth again about the House of Time. This time was a little different because the owner and a bartender remembered Sam from ten years earlier. He was still bragging about how he still had two Negro slaves.

Sam had broken the little finger of the bartender ten years prior. When he tried to debunk what Sam was telling them about the House of Time. There was no debunking him this time.

Martin did find Sam before he was too drunk to understand what Martin was telling him. After he told him what Elizabeth had said Sam looked at Martin and raised his glass as if to give a toast saying, "Let's go and kill'em!"

Meanwhile, Dulbecco and his two followers were at a seaport bordello trying to recruit women to come back to the house. They told the ladies that they were going to go into the future. However one of the women was none other than Julie. She was broke and desperate after Peter had betrayed her. So she started doing the only thing she was good at, coercing men out of their money for what she had to offer.

She recognized Louis and the other two and knew they were telling the truth. Julie saw this as an opportunity to get back on board and get even with Peter. She walked over to Dulbecco and said, "Hey I like you and you can take me in to the future. I will keep you happy for many years to come." Louis then said, "Ok I'll be glad to take but only if you can get one of this other pretty ladies to come with you."

Julie walked over to another girl, Margie, whom she was good friends with and told her, "Look Margie, I have heard of these men. They have lots of money and pay well. Forget about the time travel crap; that's just a line they say. It would be in our best interests if we go with them."

Margie took Julie's word as truth and consented to leave the bordello and go with the three men.

Marty and Henry did not know where to start looking for Peter. It was then that decided to go into all the hotels and start asking for a Peter Blake.

Elizabeth went out looking for Sidney. Her best bet was to look in the gambling houses. They were not the type of places that you would ordinarily find a prominent lawyer's wife. However, she ended up going into five of them before she found not only Sidney but Peter as well. Peter had staked Sidney the money to play with.

It was a high stakes game and Sidney was up over $4,000 dollars. Once Elizabeth had told them both about what Dulbecco had done, Sidney gathered up his money and excused himself from the game.

One man argued with Sidney about leaving with his money and not giving him a chance to win it back. But the three continued walking until the man went after Sidney. That's when Peter cold cocked the man upside the head and then the three walked out.

By six in the evening they all had arrived back at the house. Henry broke out the guns they had brought. They were far more modern then what they were accustomed to. Now it was just a waiting game. Any, and all, judgment coupled with punishment that was to be laid out was in their hands.

The big problem was the PTL, they were not sure whether to tell them for fear they might side with Dulbecco. It was therefore decided not tell them until it was over.

Martin, originally being right handed, could now only use his left arm was therefore chosen to be the last line of defense with Carson inside the house. Sidney and Peter would be inside the courtyard. Marty and Henry would be outside the courtyard hiding behind the stone wall.

A little after eight, they heard the sound of horses approaching. They were surprised to see five horses. As they came closer they could see that two of them were women.

They let them dismount before opening fire. One of the thugs was the first one to go down. Sidney proved to be useless in the gun battle. He never got off a shot. Dulbecco grabbed Margie and used her as a shield. This angered Julie. So she hiked up her long skirt and pulled out a derringer from her guarder belt. Then she shot Dulbecco in the back of the head. The other thug dropped his gun and threw up his hands.

The battle was over; but what should they do with this other thug? As Sidney and Peter came out of the court yard they saw that the one gal with the derringer was Julie.

They both had a reason to thank her and they both had reason to kill her. She still had one shot left and her gun was aimed at them. So peter said it first, "Thank you Julie."

Then Sidney followed suit. Julie moved her aim to the left and shot and killed the other thug.

Peter then jokingly said, "Problem solved!"

Martin and Elizabeth who had been hiding came out of the house. Upon seeing

Julie the atmosphere became like a family reunion. They all went inside and discussed what they all had done during the past ten years. Margie found out that the house did indeed travel through time and asked if she could stay. She knew this could give her a new start.

Later in DuPont's old room they discovered his gold and Louis's bag of cash. They split the money eight ways. Elizabeth did not want any. She was the only one that went back to Charleston. The rest of them made the trip to 1895. In private Peter gave Julie her share of the bank job.

In 1895 none of them really felt like leaving the house except young Marty; he wanted to go see his mother. She had promised that she would be there when they came back. However, this was not the case. He feared that something might be wrong. Henry and Marty got some horses from the PTL guards and headed out two their parent's home.

The rest of them discussed what they should do with the Negroes. The women agreed to let them go free. The men did not. So a compromise was drafted. The women agreed to take over the cooking and cleaning if in 1905 they would hand the Negroes a little money and give them their freedom.

The night before they were to leave again Marty and Henry returned. They reported that their mother and father were doing well. However, Elizabeth did not show up because she was having trouble with her memory. Marty felt that it might be the opium in her medicine that she had grown dependent upon.

THE YELLOW PERIL.

Charleston, South Carolina 1905

Chapter 8
The Turn of the Century

When they landed in 1905, and the windows lost their blackened state, the sun was not shining. When they opened the door there was no PLT to greet them. The sky had a layer of thick swirly clouds. They all knew that a hurricane was about to hit the coast. They scrambled around trying to find enough wood to board up the windows.

There was no talk of letting the Negroes leave. After all, they could not let them leave without a horse and a hurricane was nearly upon them. Carson was glad that they were not leaving. It was not the fact that he wanted to dominate them; but, rather he felt closer to them than the others in the house. It also concerned him that they would be going into a world that had changed.

By their estimations, if the storm did not stall, it would hit within the next twenty four hours. Fifteen hours later the storm started to come ashore. It later became known as the, no name storm of 05. It had a 16' storm surge. It battered the coast for the next twenty four hours.

Inside the house everyone was frightened. Carson had never indulged in drinking whiskey in the house before; but, on this day he made an exception. He and Peter got pretty well wasted.

Some of the cedar shingles blew off and the roof started leaking. In one area it looked like a waterfall. Two windows upstairs smashed inward from tree limbs hitting them. At times it felt like the house was going to come off its foundation. There was nothing they could do but ride it out and hope for the best.

After the storm they went out to survey the damage. The stone wall had protected the first floor of the house.

However, the upstairs showed a lot of damage. Now the question was could they get it repaired before the house jumped.

Without horses they could not even think about going into Charleston for supplies. Plus they were certain that the city would be worse off than they were.

They took all the wood and shingles they could find to repair the roof. There was no glass to fix the windows. So they boarded them up as well. Carson tried to get everything as air tight as he could. No one knew what would happen when it started to travel through time and it was not air tight. They were all aware that they might die. Carson was the one that put this fear in their head.

On the morning of September 3rd just before six o'clock they all stood in a circle in the parlor and held hands. Peter recited the Lord's Prayer. While he was praying the windows blackened. Martin glanced over at the fireplace and thought for a moment.

Then he said, "We have the fireplace burning and the wood stove going most of the time we travel and the chimneys are not making us air tight."

They all gave a sigh of relief. Then they all gave Carson a dirty look.

Chapter 9
1915

In the morning it was 1915. Two members of the PTL were there to welcome them and the storm was not. Once again they received a newspaper and a list of events that happened while they were gone.

Marty and Henry left to go and see if they could still locate their parents. Margie asked if she could tag along. Margie had told Julie that if Henry was not going to take the first step toward a relationship then she would take it for him.

After the three of them left Julie said, "It's time to set the Negroes free."

The Negroes were told they were free, and, as they had agreed, gave them each a horse and some money. Carson said he would take them into town and show them were the other Negros lived. So it finally came to pass, fifty years after the Civil War that Jacob and Esther were now free.

As the two brothers and Margie approached the city they could not believe their eyes. Horseless carriages were everywhere as well as something called the light bulb. The House of Time still used whale oil for light.

When they reached the address of their parent's home they discover it was now only an empty lot. It was over grown with trees and brush. Their hearts sunk deep into their chest. They weren't sure who to turn to for information.

Henry said, "Let's go over to father's law office and see if he is there!"

Marty agreed and off they went. At first they were relieved to see that their father's name was still on the sign. However after they went in they learned the truth. Elizabeth and Edward Sr. died in the no name storm of 05 when the house collapsed on them. Edward's law partner then handed the boys the deed to the empty lot.

The shock of losing their folks was almost too much to bear. They realized that they were now alone in the world. The House of Time was all they had left. Margie was glad that she was there to comfort Henry. She placed her arms around him and held him close. The three no longer wanted to explore the year of 1915 so they returned to the house.

The wagon they were riding in was slowly traveling down the rough country road toward their secluded house. Up ahead they notice a woman carrying a suit case to large for her to handle. As the woman heard the wagon approach she turned and waved them to stop. The tired young female then said, "Could you please extend me the favor of taking me as far as you are traveling."

Marty gazed at the woman who wore tattered clothes and had somewhat matted hair and said, "We are traveling quit a long way but we shall be glad to take you part way."

"Just take me as far away from this place as you can."

After she was in the wagon there was a round of introductions and the three found out that her name was Janet.

"May I ask Janet, for what reason are you leaving Charleston?"

"I'm getting away from my abusive father and brothers. I'm going to start a new life somewhere far away."

Overlooking her immediate appearance Marty found her very attractive. Then Marty asked, "If you could travel say ten years into the future would you?"

"Oh you're talking about the legend of the traveling house. Well if it were true I would not hesitate going in."

"Is that so? We have a very large house and we would be happy to feed you and put you up for the night."

Then Margie said, "Yes please come spend the night with us."

Janet knew that if she did not except the offer she would be sleeping in the woods. So she accepted their invitation. Janet then spoke up and said, "You mentioned that you were traveling a long ways?"

Henry quickly said, "Yes but not for a few days."

Marty explain that they lived some distance off the main road and not to worry. They would bring her back in the morning. Shortly after turning off the main road, there was a PTL member standing guard. He recognized them so he just waved them on. They did not have to stop and recite the entrance phrase. Janet simply thought he was a neighbor saying hello.

Once they arrived back at the house, Janet saw a home that was badly in need of repair. However, when she walked in, she was totally amazed at how lavish the interior was.

Marty and Henry broke the bad news of Elizabeth and Edward to Martin. Martin sank down into a chair. He knew that someday he would be faced with Elizabeth's death. However, in his time line it was just a few months ago that he married her. Martin had now lost all incentive to leave the house.

Julie had cooked dinner and it was not nearly as good as Esther's cooking. However it was palatable. During the evening meal Margie jokingly brought up the subject of the time traveling house. She told everyone that Janet said if the legend was true she would stay forever.

Julie then spoke up and said, "Janet we could use an extra pair of hands around here cooking and cleaning. Would you be willing to stay and help out for a few weeks for room and board?"

"Yes I'd be happy to, as long as you do not tell anyone in town where I am."

Then Peter, in his half drunken state, said, "Oh don't worry no one will ever find out where you've gone."

Marty was delighted that she was staying on. Later Martin pulled his Marty aside and asked, "Son do you think it is wise to bring her along without her knowledge."

Marty could not bring himself to call Martin father seeing how he was only six years older than he was.

"She would not believe us even if we tried to tell her the truth."

A bad precedent had just been set in motion. On the morning of September 3rd Marty was the only one to get up early. He was patiently waiting for Janet to come down so he could explain the blackened windows.

That morning the house faced two problems, Janet and the PTL. The house was about to land right in the middle of what was called prohibition. On the surface that would only upset Peter. However, the PTL saw this as away to make money by the use of several stills. They located them on the 500 acres. This attracted a different type of member to the Secret Society. The members started to become more crime orientated.

Janet came down the elegant staircase to which the others had grown accustomed to.

Her eyes became fixed on the blackened windows. Marty had been thinking all morning on how to tell her the truth and what her reaction might be. He would now find out.

Over the past week Marty had fallen head over heels in love with Janet. Julie and Margie had given her a complete makeover. Once she had gotten cleaned up and in proper clothing she was a very attractive lady. Marty's palms were sweaty and his selfish joke was about to be exposed.

As Janet starred at the window she said, Oh my God, what has happened?"

Marty started fumbling for words to say. However, Janet could not contain herself and burst into laughter.

Martin with a confused look said, "You knew!"

"Yes, Julie and Margie convinced me days ago that the house was real."

"And you choose to stay?"

"Yes, I chose to stay with you."

Marty gently walked toward Janet and opened his arms and she leaped into them and they had an exceedingly long kiss.

Chapter 10
1925 Roars

Later that morning Carson opened the door. There stood seven members of the PTL. This worried Martin because he was aware that only three members at a time were to actually know about the house. Marty, Henry, Margie and Janet were excited about going out to explore. They were all overwhelmed when they saw that they would be taken into town in an automobile. They were informed that it was called a Ford Model T.

The rest of them were reading the list of events that had taken place over the last ten years when Sidney yelled out, "What, women have the right to vote. What the hell is the country doing?"

A few seconds later Peter screamed, "What's this probation on alcohol crap?

How can I get whiskey now?"

Carson over heard the mention of no whiskey and asked, "Are the taverns still open?"

Carson did not know what the paper said. It did sometimes frustrate him that he could not read.

A man by the name of Rodger who was with the PTL spoke up and said, "Well Sir you folks can come on down to the lodge and ya'll can drink and there's always a poker game going on."

Only one of the seven PTL members that showed up that morning was a key member. Key members were the only ones to be allowed to see the house. It was also in the by-laws that no key member would tell any house guest about the lodge.

This was set up this way by DuPont. So no other members would socialize with the guests. A man by the name of Rodger was not a key member and had no right even seeing the house. However Joe Billings a key member had made a wager that he could prove the House of Time was real. Basically he sold the secrecy of the house for money. Billings realized that things were about to get out of hand and there was not much he could do to stop it.

Rodger then turned and said, "You fellows follow me I'll drive yea."

Sidney noticed that he had a bad limp in his left leg and asked him why. Rodger replied saying, "Oh, I got this one in the big one."

Sidney did not want to appear stupid so he let the answer slid by without further explanation. The two brothers with their girl friends rode into downtown Charleston on cloud nine. Their joy in riding in an auto was only heightened by their expectations of what was to come.

They saw a movie theater and found out that photographs now moved. Light bulbs have replaced whale oil and bicycles also have motors. They were all very tempted to stay in this time period. However, as they strolled down the sidewalks they felt like freaks in a side show. Their clothing was

very outdated. People would stare and snicker at them. Their choices were simple either go home or buy new threads. Thanks to Dulbecco and DuPont, Marty and Henry had the money to take the girls shopping.

In dealing with people they soon discovered that Charleston had changed immensely. The people were not as kind or at all friendly. Janet was shocked at just how much things were different than ten years ago. This was the point, when they all decided they would remain time travelers.

At the PTL lodge Carson once again could not keep his mouth shut. The more he drank the more he bragged. His loud mouth attracted the attention of a gang of men wanted by the law for robbery and murder. The five criminals were all PLT members that had been hiding out in the 500 acres. They saw this as a great opportunity to evade the law. Therefore, at nine o'clock in the evening of September 2, 1925 the five showed up on the doorstep of the House of Time.

Their guns were drawn and they demanded passage on the next trip into the future. Martin who had assumed the role of man in charge had little choice but to allow them in.

They were part of a sinister group which was established and designed to spread fear throughout the Black population that still lived in the southern states. This was the KKK. Only WASP's could be members of the KKK; White Anglo-Saxon Protestants. It is a common myth that the KKK targeted only the Blacks. They also hated the Jews, Catholics, liberals etc.; but, most of their hatred was directed against the poor black families in the south who were very vulnerable to attack.

To say that the KKK was a violent organization is an understatement. They spread terror through the South. The white-hooded KKK burnt churches of the black population, murdered, raped, and castrated. They were rarely caught as most senior law officers in the South were high ranking KKK men or sympathetic with their aims: to create a white-protestant south.

Even white people who had contacts with the blacks had reason to fear the KKK. It was the new traveler's goal to insure that the KKK continued their reign of terror in the future. Carson was the only one sympatric to their cause.

Chapter 11
1935

All five gang members left the morning of August 27, 1935. Their intention was to wreak more havoc upon the black population. The other travelers were all glad to see them leave and to find out about the repeal of the 18th amendment. Of course Peter was especially interested because he continued to stay drunk.

In the morning the rest of the traveling group was standing outside in the courtyard when they saw their first airplane. At first they saw it as a large silver bird. You can only imagine their disbelief to see this flying machine. All of them felt more and more out of place and disconnected with society. There was always that hope that one more jump would set things right.

More disappointment set in when the five gang members returned. They had raised hell with the area Blacks. The five had even gone so far as to hang three Black men for no reason.

Four more men pushed their way into the house to travel to 1945. They also were undesirable members of the corrupted PTL.

In 1945 only the nine members of the PTL went into town. However, the other nine guests were dumb struck to read that over 60 million people died in what was called World War II. It was questioned just how many people were left in the world.

When the nine thieves and murders returned to jump into 1955 they brought one more asshole with them. The PTL called the nine others in the house the old ones. Martin, Peter, Sidney, Carson, Marty, Henry, Julie, Margie and Janet were fed up. They all had regrets getting on board this never ending Merry-Go-Round. Deep down they all knew they could never get off and lead a normal life ever again.

The miracle of the house had become a curse and a hideout for criminals. Bridges and DuPont would roll over in their graves if they knew what their creation had succumb too. Martin was so distraught that he was the first one of the group to consider suicide.

By this time the legend of the house had traveled around the world. Most of course did not believe that such a house existed. But what a shock they all had when the house landed and opened the door in 1955.

There were at least a hundred people outside the courtyard. All were PTL members. However, many had their wives and some even had their children with them. It was like a zoo and the guest of the house were the cadged animals. The nine PTL members walked outside and waved like it was a welcome home party.

The old ones felt disgusted and were totally afraid to go out the door. Carson closed the door. Then he turned and looked at the others and said, "Now what are we going to do?"

Martin spoke up and said, "I don't know about the rest of you but I'm tired of all this. I never wanted this kind of attention. When Elizabeth and I moved in here we did not fully understand what we were getting ourselves into. We simply thought it would be a short adventure and things would return to normal when we came out."

There family fortunes were long gone. None of them had trade skills that would get them a job to earn money. They were all truly frightened with the prospect of having to go out of the house and into this unknown world.

Martin walked over and poured himself a shot of whiskey. This was highly out of character for him. He threw it down his throat and said, "I don't want to live anymore."

The others were more taken back by the shot of whiskey rather than what he had just said. Sidney spoke, "Perhaps this is the end of the line for all of us."

Janet would later be quoted as saying, "I'm sure if we stay in the house everything will be fine!"

No one really believed that. They assumed they were doomed no matter what they did.

Meanwhile, the new leader of the PTL took the nine members that had just traveled over to the lodge. The leader's name was Ray. Ray Clayton, the meanest man in the South. At least that's how he wanted people to think of him.

He said, "Look here boys we are going to give you folks a going away party on September 2nd and a lot of the people are just going to party all night and won't leave until the next morning. You understand what I'm saying. Some are going to know what is going on and some are not."

"I don't think so Clayton, not this time. You see this is our chariot and nobody is going for a ride unless I say so."

"I'm sorry you feel that way boys. But yea see here I came prepared in case you gave me that answer."

Ray looked over to a darkened corner of the lodge and waved his arm for someone to come over. A large man stood up and as he got closer to them you could see he was in a uniform. A sheriff's badge hung above his left shirt pocket.

"Sheriff it would seem that I have stumbled across some wanted fugitives of the law."

"Is that right, Mr. Clayton?"

At that moment all the men in the lodge pulled out guns and aimed them at the nine.

"Well just a minute Ray! I believe I have changed my mind about that party."

"It's too late for that! Take them away Sheriff and lock them up."

Then with a big smile on Ray's face he said, "Then bring me the key."

Back at the house Julie told the men that she needed food and other supplies. No one really felt like going. But then Henry opened up and said, "Marty and I will go!"

Well that was the last thing Marty wanted to hear. So he fired back with, "No I won't, and you cannot make me!"

Carson rolled his eyes and said, "I'll go with you!"

By this time some of the people that were still outside had climbed the gate and were now peering into the windows. Margie and Janet went around closing the drapes. Then they started knocking at the door to be allowed to come in the house.

Martin walked over to the door with another shot of whiskey in his left hand and yelled, "I have a gun and I'm not afraid to use it. Go away now or I will."

They did stop knocking but did not leave the courtyard. Henry then spoke up, "It looks like going to the market is out!"

They spent the next five days secluded in their tomb of doom. On their fourth day Martin spent three hours on the corner of his bed with a pistol in his mouth. He was trying to get up the courage to end his life of torment. The others never knew how close he had come to pulling the trigger. What stopped him was a stupid reason. He knew that they could not go outside a bury him. So therefore he would become a burden.

On the fifth day there was another person at the door. It was Ray Clayton. He yelled in that he had supplies. They were all excited because this was an answer to their problem. Food had become scarce. It was however not the answer they were looking for. It simply made the situation worse. As

Ray entered the house he brought with him a group of men carrying boxes. Then he said,

"These are the supplies for the party tomorrow night."

Julie was noticeably upset and said, "What party?"

"We are having a going away party for you folks. I thought the other fellows had told you before they got arrested."

Martin commanded, "We have never had such a party before and we do not want one now! Besides, the less people who know about this house the better."

"Well, like it or not, you're getting one and you'll say nothing more or out you go. Is that clear?"

Martin turned and walked over and once again poured a shot of whiskey. Then Peter said, "Pour one for me as well."

It would seem that as long as Ray was alive he would be in charge. There was a silver lining to all this; the other nine would not be coming back. However, this did strike fear into the others. If they left the house they too would be arrested.

Even though only three months had past for them, most of the nine had traveled in the house now for 110 years. That would make Sidney the oldest man alive at 165.

However, it wasn't their ages but rather how they got that old that mattered. Many saw the house as a fountain of youth. However, Martin and the other eight would tell you that it was anything but that.

At six in the evening four armed guards stood outside the courtyard as guests of the party started to arrive. The nine couldn't even hope to socialize with this crowd. Their clothing alone made them stand out. However, their inability to communicate and understand the people living in the 1950s was frustrating to all.

Clayton then took the time to talk to Martin. "Mr. Hopkins you are to be in charge of the house when I am not here. If anyone was to ask you about the house you are to tell them that the house is used to give criminals a new start. Is that clear?"

"Yes I will do that!"

A fellow by the name of Billy Bob showed up with another man that was obviously already drunk. Billy-Bob was Ray Clayton's brother-in-law.

"Ray, you are not going to believe who I got with me."

"Who's that Billy Bob?"

"The factory rep, Jake, of that company you hate. You know, that damn Yankee Company that had stolen the contract from your cousin's company in Savannah. When he does not show up tomorrow they're going to wish they had not used those Cleveland people."

"Well thank you Billy Bob, stick him in a room and by the time he wakes up it will be 1965."

All total there were about sixty people at the party. Plus, some had brought their children. As the evening wore on and the more alcohol that was consumed the more people committed to abandoning their old life and starting a new one.

Eleven of the party guests made the jump. One of them was a child and one was Jake the factory rep from Cleveland. He was the one Billy Bob pulled the dirty trick on.

Long about five o'clock the couple that had brought the child came back to the house. Everyone assumed that Martin was the Inn keeper.

"Pardon me Mr. Hopkins, I am Paul Green and this is my wife Molly and, of course, our son Henry. We have been out exploring all day and we were wondering what time tomorrow will we be returning to 1955."

"Returning? My good man we are not going back!"

"But Mr. Clayton said we were."

"This house only goes forward in time. Not backwards!"

"Then how do we get back? We have friends and family, a house, a job!"

"You don't! You start over again!"

"Mr. Hopkins, if Clayton has not died in the last ten years, I swear to you that I will kill him."

"Mr. Green I pray you do."

The family walked out and Martin never saw them again. After a run in with the man Jake, who had slept off his drunkenness in the room upstairs, Martin became exceedingly sickened by this house of evil. It was just another reason why he wanted out.

The one good thing that the PTL had done was run a water line to the courtyard because their well had run dry. They all were amazed by this invention. It would be the closest they would ever get to indoor plumbing.

Only two of the eleven unwanted ones returned to make the next jump. That was Tony and Robin Thomas. Tony and Robin were young and both had hated their jobs at the drive-in theater. Martin did his best to talk them out of it. But they kept saying they had nothing to lose and everything to gain. The real truth was that they were not married.

Robin was the type of woman to wear clam diggers and flats. Poodle skirts, that were so popular in the 50s, were not her thing. Tony smoked Lucky Strikes and wore his black hair in a spit curl. Blue jeans and pointed toed shoes were his dress code. Plus, he knew that in any day he was going to get his draft notice.

After their next leap they learned that in 1965 learned that another President had been assassinated. They also learned that a man by the name of John Glenn had gone into outer space and circled the earth three times in just five hours. The nine old ones could not even comprehend this event. After all they could not even understand a telephone.

Chapter 12

1975

When they arrived in 1975 a large portion of the ten-foot-stone wall had collapsed. The PTL had not been maintaining things. However, they found out that Ray Clayton and two other PTL members had been murdered. There now was a man by the name of Rick Landers in charge.

Rick had taken the funds of the PTL and was running a loan shark business. One way or another most of the PTL were involved. They had their illegal loans out to many individuals as well as numerous small businesses.

Martin and Marty went to see Rick and asked him to repair the wall. He said he would get his men right on it. But it had not been repaired by the time they left. Rick did manage to sell four tickets for a ride in the house. He got $5,000 from each person. All four were wanted by the law for various crimes.

Another startling event they learned was that man had traveled to the moon and back. Not knowing anything about space suits they simply believed there was air on the moon.

Other than the two going to see the leader of the PTL in the lodge, none of the old ones left the house. A deep, mental depression was rearing its ugly head.

There were now fifteen people that were scheduled to travel to 1985. Julie was not pleased that she had to cook for so many people. She had always tried to make the evening meal on the night they were traveling a special one.

The regular traveling men had all gained weight due to lack of exercise and good food. Margie and Janet were kept busy letting out their clothing. The consumption of whiskey by the men had also substantially increased. Even the women were nipping at the bottle.

Three of the men that had paid to travel into the future were making advances toward Julie. She did not understand all that they were saying but she did pick up on the fact that they were quit vulgar. Tony and Robin were more aware of what the men were all about; and, therefore they had a greater sense of fear of them.

Sidney, having been born in 1799, knew that he had no right to still be alive. There was one thing that he had never confessed and that was that his birthday was September 2nd. Julie, having at one time been his wife, knew that; but, never said a word. Sidney could have celebrated his birthday every week.

Two other secretes were being kept by Margie and Janet. It seems that both of them felt that they were pregnant. Neither one of them knew how Marty or Henry would take the news. However, they both confided the information to Julie. One thing was certain and that was if they decided to stay in the house it would be centuries before they gave birth.

So it was that at 6 a.m. on September 3, 1975 the fifteen left and in twenty-four hours they would be in 1985. This was the year the PTL unraveled.

In 1983 the FBI had had enough with the PTL. They knew about their racketeering, drug running, prostitution and loan sharking. The FBI needed to get more evidence to bring them down.

The FBI was able to get three uncover agents into the Secret Society. One of them became a key member. However, the agent did not believe the bull crap about the House of Time even though he had heard the legend.

Over time Rick Landers had to go further and further underground to hide himself from the watchful eyes of the law. The key members and their lieutenants were forced to meet in the early hours of the day. Using the lodge as a cover for their meetings was ideal.

The FBI agent that was the key member of the team had a code name of Jimmy. His job was to wait until there was enough evidence against Rick before bringing the hammer down. Jimmy alone would decide when and where that would happen. These were his instructions and for the last ten months he had no contact with the FBI.

In just a few days the house would reappear in 1985 and the members of the

PTL couldn't care less. At the same time Jimmy was about to call in the cavalry to make all the arrests.

On August 27th, the same day the house was to appear, Jimmy was told that there would be another major meeting of all the PTL leadership on Tuesday morning September 3, 1985. He was also expected to be at the lodge by 5:00 a.m. Jimmy broke the silence and contacted his superiors at the FBI to set up the sting. Plans were then made to raid the lodge on Tuesday morning September 3rd.

The house became visible without fanfare. No one was there to greet them. The four unwanted guest that had paid to make the trip were forced to walk. They hoofed it all the way out to the main road to see about getting a ride back into town. The others made up their minds that they were going to stay in their self-imposed prison.

All of them except Tony and Robin were in a deep state depression. They wanted all this to end but feared going to the authorities. Tony and Robin were only upset because there was no easy way into town. Martin and the others could not help but notice the wall was never repaired. They interrupted this neglect as a sign that the PTL no longer existed. This meant they were truly on their own.

Jimmy arrived at the appointed time of 5 a.m. September 3rd. Cars began arriving with other top crime figures of the PTL. Rick was always the last to arrive. Dale Nelson, the other key member, had shown up at the same time as Jimmy. It was their job to take roll call and set the stage for Rick's arrival.

Five minutes after Rick had gotten there the FBI moved in. Outside the lodge the gun battle started with the guards. Even though Jimmy was inside, he could not make a move. The others were too heavily armed. Dale and Rick and three others ran out the back door and headed for the woods. Jimmy's job was to stay with Rick so he followed them.

One of the FBI agents drew a bead on one of them and shot him dead. Rick, Dale, Jimmy, and two of the lieutenants fought their way through the thick and rough under brush. The thorns were like razorblades. One of them hooked Jimmy in the corner of his left eye. Rick's destination was the House of Time which was scheduled to leave in just a few more minutes.

Jimmy knew he had to out run the agents that were in pursuit or else he would succumb to friendly fire. In the early morning hours it was not easy to find the path leading to the house because of the heavy fog. The two lieutenants were falling behind the other three. As they ran Jimmy could see that there was indeed a house behind a stone wall.

At that moment the three heard gun fire. The lieutenants were mixing it up with the FBI and there was no way to know the outcome of the gun battle.

Rick climbed over the broken part of the wall and ran toward the door. In just a few moments the house was going to leave. Jimmy, Rick and Dale started pounding on the door in hopes of entering.

Everyone inside, with the exception of Tony, had no intention of opening the now locked and sealed door. Tony asked, "Hey man, aren't you going to open the door?"

"No!" said Martin. "We are just a few seconds from leaving. We can't risk opening it."

Just then Rick yelled out, "Help! Let us in."

Tony ran to the door and proceeded to open it. Carson hurried over to stop him but he was too late. When the door flung open the three key members of the PLT lunged in. Carson then helped Tony close and seal the door shut. Seconds later the windows blackened.

Outside the two FBI agents that had been following them were making tracks toward the house when it disappeared. One of them stopped and said, "Did you see that?"

"See what?

"That house just disappeared!"

The other agent said, "Are you crazy, what house? All I see is an over grown cemetery."

Had Jimmy, the undercover FBI agent, known what he was stepping into he certainly would not have followed them into the house. He had a wife and a three year old son. Since taking this assignment he has had only limited contact with them. Now he was going to be gone for ten years.

However, he was not aware of that yet. He still believed that within seconds the FBI was going to come barging in. It was then that he started looking around at the room he was in. He saw a beautiful, well-persevered home that was very dated. It still had oil lamps for lighting, but it was lavishly decorated. Yet, from the outside it looked like an old, worn-out house. The house still had oil lambs for lighting.

Then he saw the other occupants and how they were dressed. At this point he was starting to fear the legend was true. When Jimmy finally came to the realization that he was traveling through time he also became exceedingly depressed.

Rick and Dale on the other hand were exceedingly glad. They had escaped the clutches of the FBI and they were on the 1995 express.

Chapter 13
Another Part of the Country

In the summer of 1995 there was a TV show that was called; "Legend and Myth Seekers". It was hosted by Derik Post and Patricia Wells. It had been on the air for five years and in the past the show had enjoyed good ratings. However, the ratings were slipping and the revenues were down. They needed a low cost show, one that was close to home and not halfway around the world. They needed a myth or legend that they could push all summer for the upcoming fall season.

The producer of the show had known about the legend of the House of Time for quite some time. However, nothing could be done until the house was supposed to come back in the fall of 1995.

Well that time had finally come and they all got very excited over the project. It would be their perfect opening show.

In their preliminary investigation it was discovered were the house was to appear. The location was a 500 acre, wooded area just outside the city of Charleston. The land was once controlled by the PTL, a secret crime organization. However, now it was owned by the county for back taxes. There was talk about using the land to expand the city airport.

Next they had to try and find out the exact date that it would reappear. They ran ads in the local newspapers asking for any one that had creditable info on the dates of the legendary house to call in. You can imagine the number of crackpot calls they received.

However, one date that was mentioned most was August 27th. But then they hit the mother lode.

"This is William Bale! I am a retired FBI agent and I saw the house disappear right before my eyes."

At this point Miss Patricia Wells got on the phone and asked, "When was this sir?"

"The morning of September 3, 1985, I'll never forget that date. Everyone in the department thought I was crazy, especially when I put it in my report. That is when my name changed to Crazy Bill."

"What report was that William?"

"It was when we busted the PTL crime organization."

"What does PTL stand for?"

"The Protectors of the Light is what I was told."

"What light would that be?"

"I have no idea!"

"Can you show us where you saw the house?"

"I'd be glad to; maybe if you can find the house then I can clear my name."

According to the legend they were told that the house would be there in a location for one week. When the TV people backed up the date of September 3 they came up with August 27th. That was the date that was reported most by the call-in.

After going to the site with Crazy Bill, Derik and Patricia went to see the FBI. At first the FBI was not interested until they realized that not one of three men had ever been heard from and had truly vanished without a trace. However, they would only commit to saying maybe they would send agents to the scene on August 27th.

As expected the TV studio promoted the show all summer long. It seemed like the whole nation had gotten excited. Many citizens wanted to know the location of the house. But the producer wanted it kept a secret. However, somehow at the last moment the word got out as to its landing position just outside Charleston.

The producer came to Patricia and Derik and said, "Derik we have decided to bring in a helicopter and we want you in it and Pat will cover the story from the ground."

"No way, I will take the ground; Pat can fly! She cannot handle the ground interviews."

"Sorry, it's a done deal. You will take to the air and Pat will take the ground."

"Yeah, but Pat will get to do all the interviews if there is a house."

"Oh well, like I said before Derik, sorry."

Inside the house tension seemed a little high. There were more unwanted guests and these men were armed and had guns drawn. Marty, Margie, Henry and Janet had slept in that morning and were unaware of the dangerous men downstairs. To relieve any and all tension Martin calmly said, "You can put your guns away. No one here will hurt you."

Rick then waved his gun at everyone and said, "Everyone shut up and sit down."

Peter walked over and poured himself a whiskey. Julie spoke up and asked, "Would anyone like breakfast?"

Sidney replied, "Yes I would and it's too early to start drinking."

Robin said, "I'll help you Julie."

Then she walked into the kitchen with her.

Rick was no longer feeling in control and this was confusing to him. The old ones had had enough of people like him and with the house in general. They would just a soon be dead as to go on.

Marty and Janet woke up and were doing some pillow talk when she decided to tell Marty about being pregnant. She put her figure on his chest and started twisting it around in a circle and said, "Marty, you're going to be a father." He then laid flat on his back and starred at the ceiling. In a whispering voice said, "You do realize that if we stay in the house you will be expecting for centuries."

"I don't care what goes on out there it will still only be nine months in here."

"Yes as long as this lot we land on stays empty!"

"Oh dear, I never thought of that! What would happen if they built something here?"

"No one knows."

Robin lit the wood stove while Julie got ready to cook eggs and sausage. She planned on cooking a lot of food. She understood that when the smell of her cooking reached the rest of the house more would come eat.

Jimmy was the first to put his gun away. In time Dale also holstered his; however, Rick never did. It turned out that everyone ate including the four from upstairs. Marty was surprise to see Rick in the house. He had remembered him from when they went to ask about the broken stone wall.

After they ate, Marty told his father that at the age of 26 he was going to be a grandfather. Martin acted like he didn't know but Julie had already told him. Margie was upset when Henry told Marty, "Better you than me my friend."

Chapter 14
A new turn on the story

Up until this point I {Scott Franklin} have been telling you this story as to the best of my ability to piece it together. I am using facts that I had obtained and gathered from many sources. Now I will tell you how I, and why, I got involved in this pitiful, true legend.

My Part of the Story

"Thank you for calling Warren Manufacturing! How my I direct your call?"

"Yes, may I speak with Scott Franklin please?"

"One moment please!"

"Scott you have a phone call on line two."

In early August of 1995 I received a call from my real father. It had been many years since I had heard from Jake. He had abandoned my mother and me back in 1955. At that time I was only six years old. Jake never said a thing to my mother about leaving her. He just went to work and was to be gone for only three weeks. He never came home. Jake did however show up some ten years later.

Mom had already remarried a fellow by the name of Bob Simms. I like Bob; we still talk a couple times a month by phone. As far as I'm concerned, he is my dad. He is the one that took me to school and church. He is the one that I played ball with and taught me about life in general. Mom passed away back in eighty-six, her death was hard on both Bob and me.

When my real father did come back to Cleveland, he became known as, "Shaky Jake" because he drank a lot. He could never hold a job for more than a few weeks. For the most part he stayed drunk and out of our lives. People on the west side of town that knew Jake thought of him as a crazy man. Many wanted him locked up in a mental ward.

Then on a Friday morning in August, I got this call from Shaky Jake. He told me that he did not have much longer to live. He wanted to see me and set the record straight about why he was gone for ten years. To be honest I did not care one way or another. However, after a few minutes on the phone with him I decided to take some vacation time and drive to Cleveland to see him. At least this way I could finally hear his side of the story.

I was forty-five and soon to be forty-six. I felt that I had waited long enough to hear what he had to say. I have been living in Iowa for some two years now. I moved here after my divorce from my wife. Now mind you, I have nothing against religion; but, one day Helen became what they call born again.

After this new revelation of God came to her, I simply did not understand Helen anymore. She was not that way when we got married. After eight years of togetherness Helen said she needed more out of life then what I could offer. She and that Bible became exceedingly too much for me to handle. As far as I was concerned being that religious was for losers and I will never be a loser. Christmas and Easter were enough church for me.

To get the facts straight, my life without Helen is at a standstill. I did not like my new life at all. Shopping for a new wife is hard work and something that I never thought I would have to do. Nevertheless, at that time, I could not see things her way. I'm now working as a sales rep for a Fortune 500 company. My boss is a good man, so when I told him that my father was dying he gladly gave me as much time off as I needed.

I left for Cleveland on Monday morning to see Jake on his deathbed. He was in intensive care at Cleveland Metro Hospital on West 25th Street. I knew the place well, that is where mom died. I checked into a downtown hotel and waited until Wednesday morning to go see the old man.

When I did arrive in his room, I did not recognize him. He was truly near death's door. He had lost a lot of weight and for the first time in a great while I was seeing him sober.

This is where the story gets strange. Jake with a weak voice told me that he did not leave mom and me by choice. He said the company that he was working for sent him to Charleston South Carolina. His company had sold quite a bit of equipment in that area to the lumber mills and they were having problems getting them set up. Jake was sent there as a troubleshooter to help them. The trip was to last only three weeks, not ten years. He stated that when he arrived in Charleston on September 2nd around noon he went right to a mill and looked over one of the problems.

Jake went on to say that, one of the good-old boys at the mill had a jar of homemade whiskey. To be sociable he sat in with all the good old boys of the mill while they passed the jar around. Therefore, before he could check into a hotel he had a little too much and became quite drunk.

He was only twenty-five at the time and said that this was the first time he had ever gotten drunk. One of the men at the mill convinced him to come to a dinner party that night. This bulldog of a man was a PTL member. I was not sure what that meant and Jake said that at the time he did not either. Jake was led to believe it was a local boarding house. He then figured he could check himself in for the night. He left the family car at the mill and rode with the bulldog named Billy Bob.

The boarding house where the man took him was called "The House of Time." Jake continued with his tall tale saying that he passed out in a room at about six o'clock that night and did not wake up until five o'clock the next morning. He then went down stairs to check out and see about getting a ride back to the mill. The house had people sleeping and passed out from the party everywhere in the house. Even on the floor in the upstairs hallway.

However, the man who ran the boarding house told him that he could not leave the house until 6 a.m. because they had not yet arrived in the future. In the meantime, they would be glad to fix him a free breakfast. Being hung over and not sure what they meant he sat down to eat. Jake said that he thought it was quite quaint that the house only used oil lamps. The man then alleged that the house was some sort of time machine. Jake maintains that when he did walk out at six o'clock the next morning it was September 3 1965 not September 3, 1955.

The cars outside had been stripped and weeds had over taken them like they had been there for years; but he had not noticed them the night before. Everything was strange and he felt out of place. He said he had no idea where he was and at one point was not sure who he was.

At first, he thought that it was the homemade whiskey that he had sucked down. So he hitched a ride to a café called the "Skyline on Market Street", to drink more coffee. Then while sitting there he read the date on the newspaper and could not believe his eyes. But after reading the paper and talking to the waitress he was convinced that it was in fact 1965.

Looking for answers, he went back to what he still believed was the boarding house. No one was there standing guard. Jake was sober this time, he looked at the house and it was a two-story, balloon style home built at least a century ago.

He proceeded back into the house to talk with the man that ran the place. They explained that it was in fact the House of Time that many legends and folklore had spoken of. He further stated that it was true the house only appeared on this lot for one week every ten years. The purpose of the house was to give certain people a second chance at life.

The keeper of the house, in an almost tearful way, said he was sorry about the mistake. However, he explained that many of their customers were people with problems and most were running from the law. Because Jake was drunk, they took mistakenly took him in.

Supposedly, a Charles Bridges built the house in 1845. He was some sort of scientist that had been chased out of England for his strange theories. The house that he built was just outside Charleston had some sort of magnetic rods running parallel through the walls. This caused the building to stay in a continued time warp. The people inside the house would only age twenty four hours and would only be aware that twenty four hours had passed.

Charles had run the house until his sudden death in 1885. A man by the name of Martin Hopkins was running the house of time now and had taken over the place after Bridges death. They told Jake that he was doing a Godly work for their Lord. With tears in his eyes, Jake told me that their work was of the devil. It ruined his life and they had let criminals go free to do more harm to others in the future. Many of the people in the house were killers that would go on killing people for decades to come.

I'm sorry that I couldn't get out of the bottle after losing you and your mother. I loved you both so very much. Please forgive me son! I do want to tell you that a few years ago, I started attending AA meetings and I finally quit drinking. Now it is too late for me to stop that evil place. I no longer have the strength to burn that place to the ground. I should have done it many years ago instead of feeling sorry for myself and staying drunk all the time.

You see this place called House of Time only appears the morning of August 27th every tenth year. It then stays visible for only a week until the morning of September 3rd. That is the only time it can be destroyed. It is going to come again in just about a week from now. At 6 a.m. in the morning of the

August 27th then it will disappear again for another ten years.

"My son please be willing to do God and me a favor and destroy that evil house. There is a man by the name of Paul Sheppard that needs your help to destroy the place. I was going to help him but as you can see, there is no way I can help him now."

"He lives in Rock Hill, South Carolina; I met him on the internet. The house ruined his life also but in a different way. His address and phone number is over there in my bag, take it with you and call him."

I was speechless for many reasons. One, the fact that Jake said he loved mom and me; two, he also had become sober. The big reason though was this crazy story about a house in South Carolina.

Who in their right mind would believe this crap; especially coming from an old drunk like him, who was close to death? After all, what did he have to lose by lying to me? Jake whispered on saying, "Some people have made many trips into the future."

He insisted that I would be amazed by the number of bad people that had been sheltered in the House of Time.

"It's witchcraft pure and simple. Humans are not meant to have that kind of knowledge. You see son, the end of time is near and this place must not continue. All these killers are going to come out this time and do a lot of bad things here and around the world. You must help Paul stop them before they all leave that house on August 27th or else there will be Hell to pay here on earth. Please take my place and help him before it is too late."

"Paul will fill you in on the details. You can trust him with your life."

Just then Jake started coughing and gasping for air. His eyes rolled back and his monitor stopped beeping and went to a flat line. A code blue was called at the nurses' station and I was told to leave the room. They brought in a crash cart and put the paddles to his chest.

A few minutes later a doctor came out and told me that my father was dead. I didn't know what to think, I had barely known the man and within an hour of his death he lays all this garbage on me.

Was he a lunatic or was all this real? There was not much that Jake told me that I could believe. However, for some reason Shaky Jake had aroused my interest concerning this house. So I went through his bag and sure enough there was an address and phone number of a Paul Sheppard.

I left the hospital and ate lunch at the hotel and called Jake's internet buddy. Over the phone, he sounded older than me. As it turned out, he was. If all that he told me over the phone was true, Paul had been through a lot more in his life than I had.

Having the time off, I decided to go to Rock Hill, South Carolina and meet this guy. I wanted to meet him face to face and see if he also was lying or if there was any truth to what Jake had told me.

While on the phone, he invited me to stay at his place. I declined. After all, he might also be a lunatic. Even I had noticed that there seemed to be more and more nut cases in this world. Paul claimed to have pictures of this place. They were said to be taken before, after and during its appearance.

He said that he had taken them himself the last time it appeared ten years ago. He also stated there were others that knew about the House of Time and wanted it kept a secret place.

Paul insisted that it was owned and operated by a secret society know as the Protectors of the Light. For short, they are known as the PTL. Even I had heard of the PTL Club but that was a Christian group. That meant "Praise the Lord!"

From what Paul had described this PTL was a far cry from being a loving group. Paul also insisted that some men that would be in this house were long time notorious criminals. These guys have been kept there under protection by the PTL for generations.

The plot was getting deeper and deeper to stand in. I felt that I had to be at this location on August 27th to see for myself whether or not this House of Time would appear. This journey was either going to be my best vacation ever or my worst ever. A few days later when I finally met with Paul he did in fact have pictures of a house in side a 10 foot stone wall.

Several other pictures showed the same courtyard without the house. It showed only a vacate lot with weeds growing. He told me that many of the town's people knew about the place. However, they refused to talk about it for fear of their lives or their families.

Paul confessed that he has changed his last name many times over the last twenty years to avoid death by the hands of the PTL. At the time Paul did not say why they were after him. He did say it was a full time job to stay one step ahead of the PTL. Paul then looked right into my eyes and asked me if I was a believer. I told him that I was not sure if I believed any of this.

We talked for a few days and he told me all about the plans that he had made with Jake. It was how they were going to go about destroying this House of Evil. Paul was really into the Bible and kept talking about the end. He said the one-world government was just around the corner. He also stated that Blacks would be hunted down and killed by these men of the PTL.

Paul stated that the people in the house were recruited to be killers and thieves. He ended up pleading with me to take Jake's place and help him carry out this mission. I agreed to go; but, for my own reasons which I did not share with Paul. I had no intention of going after wanted killers. For some reason on the day before we were suppose to leave Paul went into great detail on why he hated this place. It turns out that he was born and raised in Charleston.

He told me his father had been a higher up in another local secret society but also a good Christian man. He was told in confidence the truth about the House of Time. His father then took it upon himself to do the right thing and blow the whistle on this House of Time. He started telling people about the evil of this place and what its true purpose was.

His father not only opened his mouth about the house but also how the Governor of the state was in the PLT. Then without warning on a Sunday morning his brother, two sisters, mother and father all had their throats cut and were found hanging upside down in the family barn.

Paul stated that the Charleston Police were hot on the trail of the people that had done this to his family but were told to stop.

The police told him a command came down from the Governor's office that they alone would handle this investigation. After that there was never anything else done by anyone.

All of this happened some twenty years ago and the only reason that Paul was not executed with his family was because his father had sent him to Texas.

Paul was to tell a man by the name of Morris about the House of Time and ask for help exposing the house and who the people were that were involved with it. As it turns out, this man Morris had been helping Paul stay alive. Since the events surrounding the death of his family he has also been giving him safe places to live and work.

Chapter 15
The Big Bang

When we finally arrived in Charleston we each got a room at different motels.

This was getting interesting to me because Paul had a trunk full of dynamite. As far as I was concerned we were about to blow up an empty lot. He said it had been in the center of 500 acres all this time and we would use it as a staging area.

"Ok by me!" I thought.

The basic plan was to go to the vacant house around sunset of the 26th and about 2 a.m. in the morning spread the dynamite around where the house was supposed to appear.

The town of Charleston was, and is still, a beautiful Southern city. The people were friendly and there appeared to be a church on every corner. How could this nice place be the home of this so called evil house? It is wholesome place to live and raise a family!

We entered into the woods from the back of the property and unloaded Paul's trunk of all the goodies. He then drove his car a mile away and walked back. We sat quietly drinking coffee all night. The only sound I could hear was a train as it passed by going into town every hour all night long. Then finally 1 a.m. rolled around. Under the cover of darkness we started planting the dynamite.

I was beginning to get a sick feeling about this. Up until now it had all been a game to me. I had just wanted see if my real father was a liar or not.

It then suddenly hit me that what I was doing was illegal; I was helping to blow up a grave site. Plus, if Paul and my departed father were telling the truth about this place, then I would soon be seeking the help of the legal system to protect me.

We finished with the dynamite about 2 a.m. and went back into the woods. Then around 4:30 a.m., people started showing up. They were curiosity seekers there to see if the house was real. Some went inside the courtyard. Then around 5:30 a.m. four cars pulled up in front of the lot and were too close to us for my comfort. I was starting to believe that something was going to happen.

I asked Paul again, "Are you sure killing these people will save others?"

"I told you they deserve to die!"

"But we will have witnesses."

"That's good; we will need others to verify what we do."

Now I knew this guy Paul did not have both oars in the water. But one thing was for sure; those men out there did in fact have guns. More and more people were trampling through the woods coming to the site. At 5:40 a TV camera crew showed up and a helicopter started hovering around above our heads. This was getting too deep and I no longer wanted any part in it.

There were about a dozen people dancing around in the courtyard as if they were defying the legend. It was now six o'clock and all was not well! The ground began to rumble and a loud cracking sound was stinging my ears. Suddenly there was a bright flash of light.

It was very much the same light an arc welder produces, the kind you do not want to look at. My heart was pounding and I was certain the whole world could hear my knees knocking. After the flash I could see Patricia Wells and a few others put their hands up to their eyes and fall to the ground. Sparks flew out of the TV camera and the cameraman was forced to drop it.

"Oh my God, I thought, my poor father was right! Who in their right mind would believe this? No wonder he became a drunk. I looked over at Paul and he was about ready to throw the switch to blow up the house. There was no way I could let him do that. I leaped over and pushed him away from the trigger.

He fought back. I discovered rather quickly that he could hit pretty hard.

To put a fast end to the silly struggle I picked up a rock and forced his head to become intimate with it. After that blow to the head he went down. Later that morning it took a paramedic to revive him.

While Paul and I had been fighting we all heard screams coming from inside the house. Apparently the people that had been standing where the house was to appear materialized into the house.

For many of them it was right below the knees. The rest of their legs were gone. They fell over onto the floor of the house and were bleeding profusely and screaming in pain. However, some were not so lucky. There were a few that materialized into the furniture or a wall. They died instantly.

The people inside the house were panic stricken. At the same time the FBI was outside yelling into a bull horn for everyone to come out with their hands up. The noise of helicopter circling above the house added to the fear and panic especially for the old ones that did not know anything about that sound.

Jimmy took advantage of the chaos to get the drop on Rick and Dale. At first Rick thought it was a joke until Dale went for his gun. Jimmy blasted it out of his hand. Jimmy then told Carson to open the door. When the door opened the sound of the helicopter got much louder. The crowd became quite in anticipation of someone coming out.

The people that had materialized in the house needed medical attention right away. Martin, Janet and Robin were all gagging and throwing up at the sight of dead and dying people throughout the first floor. Without a word being said, they all knew that it was over. Their nightmare orchestrated by the house had finally come to an end and a new nightmare was about to begin.

Sidney instinctively walked over and pulled off the board that was hiding the key. He then pulled it out so the house would no longer travel. Sidney then placed the key down the back of his pants and covered it with his coat.

Martin then walked around the dead and dying people toward the parlor desk. He reached over with his left hand and picked up his journal that he had been writing for the past 128 days; or, if you would rather me say 160, years.

Jimmy marched Rick and Dale out first. The FBI was unaware that Jimmy was on the same side. They told him to drop his weapon. He hesitated but did finally comply. Agents ran up and cuffed all three of them. Then slowly one by one in a single file the original five that had started back in 1844 and the other six travelers came walking out of the house. To their surprise as they did come out, the crowd that had gathered erupted into applauses and loud cheers.

This may not be . . . The End

Made in the USA
Lexington, KY
08 April 2013